O P W C B
A T E Z U
N O B Y L
C T V I L

For Ari and Eliot, who inspired "Donny" and who helped to make him real, and for everyone out there who stands up to bullies.

First published in 2017 by Julia Levy

ISBN 978-0-692-83451-0

First edition

The author/illustrator used cut origami paper and newsprint to create the illustrations for this book.

Printed in China

Set in Amatic

Design by Ari Edelson

DONNY the BULLY

Julia Levy

Thanks for
joining the
campaign!
Julia Levy

Donny's fingers go "click"
In the deep of the night.
He is feeling SO mad —
In the mood for a fight.

"She helped those guys beat us.
They scored — Run, Run, Run!
Because Carly can't catch,
Our season's all done."

"It's SAD she can't run fast!
She lost the whole game!
She failed us completely.
          It's Carly I blame."

Donny's finger clicks "send."
His face twists to a smirk,
And he says to himself,
"I KNOW this will work."

"If a player's no good,
And can't play the game,
We should shout it out loud,
And put her to shame."

Carly reads Donny's words,
And just wants to scream.
"What gives HIM the right?
We lost as a team.
What he wrote isn't true!
What he said isn't right!"

But for Donny, mean words
Are his greatest delight.

At school, will they know?
Will the mean words have spread?
Will they all be against her?
Carly's mind fills with dread.

At her locker she finds
A note scrawled in black.
It is Donny again —
He is on the attack.

The whispers are spreading
All over the school.
She feels all alone.
Oh! That Donny's SO cruel.

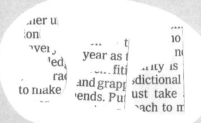

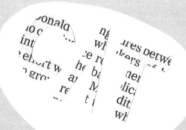

In class, Carly's silent,
At the sound of her name.
She runs to the bathroom,
Her face red with shame.

"I LOST THE WHOLE GAME.
I'M AN EXPERT AT FAILING.
I'M SLOW AND I'M USELESS,"
SAYS CARLY CAT, WAILING.

"IT'S MY FAULT — I KNOW IT.
I HAVEN'T BEEN TRYING.
I HAVE TO WORK HARDER.
HE'S NOT EVEN LYING!"

Then she hears a loud "knock,"
And a voice saying, "Hi."
"It's Lily, your friend.
Please, try not to cry."

"Carly," says Lily, "his post was obscene.
Everyone knows that Donny is MEAN.
We played as a team,
We lost it together.
It's not all your fault.
We should ALL have done better."

"I've got something to show you:
A new viral graphic,
I've never — in life —
Seen this kind of traffic."

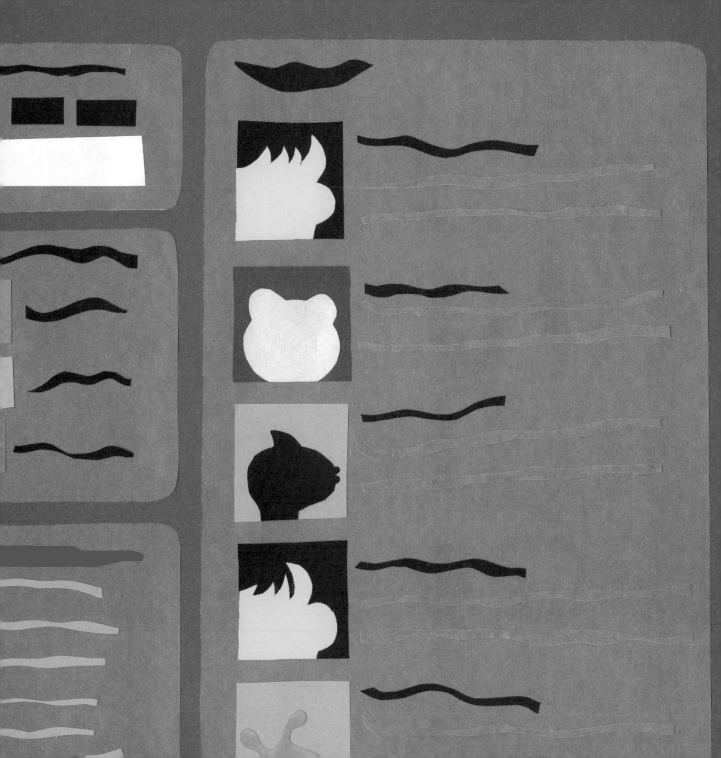

Lily Frog stands up straight,
Green, tall, and serene.
She holds out her phone.
Carly looks at the screen.